Praise for *Syllables of Rain*

"Llewellyn is devastated after his girlfriend walks out on him. Cookie is on his own after his wife kicks him out of the house. Llewellyn and Cookie, two former homeless Vietnam vets, meet again by chance in Baltimore. All the members of their little group are dead, including Jansen, who tried to help them find balance in their lives through Zen Buddhism. Llewellyn, attempting to track down his spiritual path through recalling his past, has returned to Baltimore only to find it much changed. Cookie, dealing with his despair through drink, is sinking fast. As they work through their conflicting issues, the two men realize what they must do to keep the hope for their futures alive. *Verdict*: Lliteras (*Viet Man*) has created a compact, emotionally charged snapshot of two soldiers trying to make sense of the world around them. Combining prose and poetry, this slim novel will leave a lasting impression on anyone who is or has known a military veteran."

—*Library Journal*

"*Syllables of Rain* is a brilliant work of pure genius by D.S. Lliteras . . . My favorite kind of Vietnam War book is short, poetical, and filled with hard-fought truths . . . This is that book. Distilled from the water of a career of writing books like nobody else can write, D. S. Lliteras has brought his unique genius to bear on the world of the Vietnam veteran . . . *Viet Man* was the gritty in-country novel, but *Syllables of Rain* is the poetic novel of a lifetime of coping with war, of struggling to make peace with Vietnam . . . I'd thought that D. S. Lliteras' previous book, *Viet Man*, was untoppable, but I was dead wrong. His new book did the trick and more besides."

—*The VVA Veteran*

"D.S. Lliteras' approach in this brave new novel is both very Miles (as in Davis) and also very Kerouac (as in the Beat Generation novel, *The Dharma Bums*). *Syllables of Rain* is a book that delivers what is most artful and true in Lliteras' writing."

—*The MacWire (TMW) Worthy Entertainment & Celebrity News*

Syllables

of

Rain

a novel

D.S. Lliteras

RAINBOW RIDGE
BOOKS

Cover and interior design by Frame25 Productions
Cover photograph © Grisha Bruev c/o Shutterstock.com

Published by:
Rainbow Ridge Books
140 Rainbow Ridge Road
Faber, Virginia 22938
434-361-1723

If you are unable to order this book from your local
bookseller, you may order directly from the distributor.

Square One Publishers, Inc.
115 Herricks Road
Garden City Park, NY 11040
Phone: (516) 535-2010
Fax: (516) 535-2014
Toll-free: 877-900-BOOK

Library of Congress Cataloging-in-Publication Data
applied for.

ISBN 978-1-937907-52-5

10 9 8 7 6 5 4 3 2 1

Printed on acid-free recycled paper
in the United States of America

Dedicated to Kathleen Touchstone

"Talk not to me of blasphemy, man;
I'd strike the sun if it insulted me."
—Herman Melville, *Moby-Dick; or, The Whale*

*"We have art so that we shall not
be destroyed by the truth."*
—Friedrich Nietzsche

Contents

CHAPTER 1

Keeping Secrets

Life with Sandy did not work out.

Love does conquer all things, but love does not necessarily make a person happy. At least, that's what she told me when she stood in the living room with her bags packed and her emotions wrapped.

She left the apartment without slamming the door.

Okay. We needed better furniture. Okay. We needed more money. Okay. I did not or could not share with her the emotions that she wanted from me.

She thought I was keeping secrets from her. She thought there was a place inside of me that she could not reach.

Okay. She was right. But I had no control over that. I wasn't doing anything wrong, and I wasn't doing what she thought I was doing on purpose.

Okay. There was darkness inside of me. Okay. Darkness.

folding my hands
before facing loneliness;
when does it start?
when does it end?

CHAPTER 2

Wheel of Her Regret

I walked outside wanting to leave everything behind me. But I knew I couldn't leave my job or . . . or, what? Go where? I had nowhere to go. I knew—nothing.

I was lost and alone and in need of a change. But I couldn't walk away from what was left of my present life.

I stood in the parking lot and, with each vehicle that passed by, pretended that it was Sandy at the wheel of her regret.

I stood there and bargained for her return by adding my own regret into the trunk of her car, but that didn't work because the course she was steering was set at one-eight-zero degrees and the speed she was driving was set at sixty miles per hour away from me and forever:

overcome by darkness
while standing in a parking lot;
waiting to make friends
with daybreak

CHAPTER 3

Unwanted Dreams

When I woke up from my unwanted dreams, it was still dark.

I sat up and swung my legs over the side of the bed—the floor felt cold against my bare feet. I bowed my head in defeat: I could not face daybreak standing in the parking lot in search of not being alone.

I fell back on the bed with my feet still on the floor and stared at the ceiling. I sighed. Then I closed my eyes to intensify the darkness and to reject this new cycle of my life.

> not believing the real
> to be real had become;
> not believing my dreams
> to be dreams

CHAPTER 4

French Toast

I ate breakfast at the Oasis Cafe: French toast and coffee at the counter with Keith serving and Richard in the kitchen. Keith respected my mood and let me sink into the melted butter of my silence and the hot syrup of my despondency. I smiled after taking my first bite of the French toast, covered in the melted yellow and the warm maple lake of my creation.

Keith was not fooled by my fragile change in mood. He watched my smile disappear as he poured more coffee into the half-empty cup of my black mood.

I stared at my French toast after my second bite.

She had no reason to go. She said she wasn't happy. She said she didn't know me. She said she didn't know how to rearrange used furniture.

feeling sad
for no reason;
my soul is rusty,
my heart is blue

CHAPTER 5

Empty Disposition

Coffee nerves forced me out of the Oasis and poured me onto the streets of downtown Norfolk. The autumn's breeze greeted my maple syrup after-taste—a sudden gust of wind improved my empty disposition.

It felt good to walk against the breeze and walk with the sound of traffic. It felt good to be free, to be unaccountable even to myself.

I did not know where I was going or what I was going to do when I arrived.

the synopsis of despair
intensifying the struggle;
pushed passed going
with misspelled steps

CHAPTER 6

She's Not Coming Back

I took a deep breath. I peered across the harbor at Waterside. I whispered into the wind:

"Alright. I knew this was coming. And I know Sandy. She's not coming back."

"Alright. I have mourned her loss. And I will mourn no longer, especially since it was that easy for her to leave me—the hell with it. I'm glad we did not get married."

"Alright. I need to take some leave. I have a lot of time on the books. The fire department won't miss me."

"Alright. I'll take a month off. The Chief likes me. He'll let me have it."

"Alright. Life with Jansen on the streets of Baltimore was a long time ago. I'd like to trace out some of Jansen's past. I'd like to find out what's left of him—if that's possible."

"Alright. And why not?"

Jansen had altered my sight. He had transformed my spirit. He had changed my life's orientation before he died. Perhaps seeking the past might shed some understanding light upon the things in my present.

alright to tremble
like an excited tree branch
striking the sky, yet
tangled in the clouds

CHAPTER 7

My Soul is Rusty

The heavy traffic was burdened with destination. I was tired by the time I reached Baltimore.

I got lost trying to find the city's inner harbor. I was surprised by all the change when I finally got there.

A significant portion of that waterfront had become the Waterside Mall. The rock and rubble adjacent to the inner harbor's seawall had been replaced by sparkling commerce. It was beautiful, but there was no past for me in there.

I drove away from the hustle of the Mall area toward one of the nearby residential districts where I discovered more change. The once-broken and abandoned row-houses had been renovated by the sweat equity labor of a middle class that now occupied them.

The homeless had gone elsewhere—probably deeper into the city where the labor of sweat equity had not yet reached.

The change was good, of course, and yet, I missed seeing these streets as they were when I was homeless and with Jansen and—

time pours into
an hourglass;
a disjointed past
strips me of my shadow

CHAPTER 8

First Cup of Baltimore

I drove until I found the corner of Light and St. Paul's Street. This intersection meant a lot to me because this corner is where my past and my present have . . . have—what? What?

I wanted coffee.

I parked my car, opened the passenger door, and stepped out into the street.

I was cold.

I slammed the door shut in response to the traffic. Once clear, I crossed the street and stepped onto the sidewalk. I veered to my left, then turned right when I reached the corner. A cold wind greeted me and forced me to blink my eyes as I continued walking.

I stopped in front of the burger joint where I once had my first cup of Baltimore coffee and pushed open its stainless steel-trimmed glass door.

I entered the joint, sat down at the counter, and ordered a second cup.

crisis heats my bloodstream
and sorrow becomes me;
perspective skims the surface
and shadows rule my empire

CHAPTER 9

Reasonable Pie

Nothing stays the same.

A pockmarked-faced boy worked the Formica-topped counter that needed cleaning. His paper hat was creased in all the wrong places.

There was no one else in the diner.

I ordered coffee.

He took his time serving me.

I didn't bother asking him about Cookie, the older man who used to work here. I could see that he didn't know anything.

He watched me take my first sip.

The thick white cup of coffee was hot and bitter.

He leaned toward me as soon as I placed the cup on its thick white saucer. "What'll you have?"

"Coffee." I ignored the young man's smirk.

"Fine." He started to walk away from the counter.

"Wait." He did not deserve my lousy disposition. "Is that apple pie?"

"Yeah."

"How about a slice?"

"Okay." The young man accepted my truce and served me a generous portion of the pie.

Strong coffee. Reasonable pie. Bad music.

I ate pie. I drank coffee.

The young man refilled my cup without my asking.

The truce was complete. The past was gone.

the absolute moment
of remembering;
lingering beyond the truth
of the facts

CHAPTER 10

This Was Real

"The present is all there is."

"What was that?" the young man in the paper hat asked. "You want something else?"

"No. Nothing."

The young man shrugged, then turned away from me to make a fresh pot of coffee. *The present is all there is*, was the first thing Jansen said to me at this counter and it is that present that remains with me now.

Strange, I thought. That present is really the past pretending to be the here and the now. But Jansen was not here. I did not want that to be true right now. Not now. Not during this moment of recognized loss that I rejected as I pushed away my plate of half-eaten apple pie.

"The pie was fresh," said the young man.

"There's nothing wrong with the pie."

The young man adjusted his paper hat. "Oh."

I placed three dollars on the counter and walked out of the burger joint.

The sound of a truck accelerating. The honk of a horn. The plaintive sound of a distant siren.

I raised my jacket's zipper against the night air. I stamped the sidewalk with my right foot. Real. Yes, this was real.

I looked at the sky and wondered if my car would be towed on a Thursday.

the silence of the moon,
this emptiness of complicity;
caught like an orphan with
empty pockets on a busy street

CHAPTER 11

The Here and the Now

The street lights projecting into the night cast angular shadows off the concrete structures of the city. I walked about feeling completely unnoticed, as if I were invisible, as if Jansen had been present.

It appeared as if sweat equity had wiped out a lot of yesterday. Many of the row-houses near the inner harbor were no longer shells of the past. Lights shining through their windows mocked my presence.

As I continued to travel away from the harbor into a nearby district, however, I discovered that there were still empty-shelled neighborhoods left to be repaired.

I felt strangely at home here because I was also a shell in need of repair. I was also a leftover from the past pretending to live in the here and the now because I couldn't forget yesterday.

Welcome to Baltimore, Llewellen, was what Jansen said to me on my first tour of this city with him.

I stopped walking and looked at the sky.

the bright falling star
did not give me peace;
if stones come from stardust,
do bright thoughts come from stone?

CHAPTER 12

Everywhere is Nowhere

I walked for a long time. My senses grew numb: sight became a blur, sound became noise, wandering became movement. Blur. Noise. Movement.

being human,
being uncertain;
why is this
a lonely business?

"I am not a bum," a man said, as I approached an intersection. He was sitting on the street curb.

"Excuse me?" I turned to him and planted myself on the sidewalk near the edge of the intersection.

"Have you got a cigarette?"

"I don't smoke."

He placed the stump of a crushed cigarette between his cracked lips. "Then what good are you?"

I reached for my wallet. "I can give you—"

"I don't want your money."

I left my wallet in my back pocket. "Okay."

"I said I'm not a bum."

"Okay." I nodded.

The man propped his elbows on his knees, then rested his forehead against the palms of his hands. "Do you have a light?"

I turned away from him, stepped off the sidewalk, and crossed the street.

angel of contempt—
feeling more
abandoned, more hurt
and alone

CHAPTER 13

Wandering Thoughts

Twilight. I kept walking. That encounter with the man sitting on the street curb disturbed me.

My mood darkened as twilight deepened into night. Uncertainty stained the corners of my past.

This quest to find Jansen was—no. This quest to find Jansen's past in Baltimore in order to find his— what? No. Not to find him. To find myself? Yes. Maybe. That's more like it. Yes. Because the truth is: for as close as I was to Jansen here, in Baltimore, I didn't know anything about him.

Sure. He was my Zen Buddhist teacher, my sensei, who was killed before he completed teaching me what he knew about Zen—if that's possible. Sure. His death left me floundering until I was able to rediscover my Western spirituality. Sure. My exposure to Jansen's brand of Eastern spirituality ultimately allowed me to appreciate my cultural religion that was Judeo-Christian—like it or not.

Anyway—who was Jansen? I didn't know. But I wasn't going to investigate his biographical past like a private detective. No. What I want to discover— no. What I want to *do* is find any spiritual legacy he might have left behind in Baltimore.

Impossible. I know.

Ridiculous. I know.

Necessary. I don't know.

I felt silly. I felt empty. I felt like a beggar burdened by wandering thoughts.

> bound for twilight's
> distant slant;
> seeking Jansen's spirit
> in this strange afterlife

CHAPTER 14

Imagined Rainbows

The beginning raindrops stained the sidewalks and the streets. I lifted the collar of my jacket to protect my neck from the syllables of rain. I decided to go back to the burger joint where I could anchor my past to a familiar nowhere.

I walked. The rain intensified.

Umbrellas magically appeared. The urban emptiness was filled with the sound of impatient vehicles traveling upon wet pavement. Raindrops glistened in midair due to headlights and street lamps and storefront incandescence.

I imagined rainbows.

vehicles polishing the boulevard,
pedestrians dodging the rain
with arabesque determination,
with apparent destination

CHAPTER 15

Its Weight Was Important

I entered the burger joint, sat on a stool, and rested my forearms on the Formica-topped counter.

I ignored the young man in the white paper hat after he served me and studied the overhead lamp reflected in my hot black coffee.

The young man had been perceptive enough to leave me alone.

I listened to the sound of small arms fire that had haunted me since the war. Within ordinary moments like this, this sound memory was often there. Within passive activities, as in sitting in theaters watching a film or ballet or a play or listening to a concert or an opera, the sound memory of distant small arms fire was often there.

This reoccurring memory was something that separated me from the protected population of American citizens; it was something that reminded me that I was once a warrior—yes. Vietnam. Its weight was important.

I shifted my position on the hard stool that I was sitting on. I watched my coffee grow cold.

eyes upon the truth
resembling condiments:
ketchup and mustard
right and wrong

CHAPTER 16

Zen Clarity

I stepped onto the wet sidewalk after I left money on the burger joint's counter beside my cold coffee and my vagrant thoughts.

Baltimore suddenly felt ugly and empty and pointless: as pointless as reading about Zen; as pointless as seeking Buddha nature and no-mind and non-attachment—all of it had become meaningless to me.

Spiritual seeking, religious achievement, Zen clarity—all, disjointed.

I've learned nothing.
I've forgotten everything.
Is there a difference?
Is there . . . .

CHAPTER 17

Hazmat Incident

"What the hell?"

The rear end of my car was destroyed. There was shattered glass and plastic everywhere. Gasoline trickled onto the street from my car.

I did not see another damaged vehicle.

I approached the police officer who was investigating the scene. He appeared to be estimating the amount of fuel that was pouring out of the broken gas tank.

The police officer saw me approaching him. "Is this your vehicle?"

"Yes, it is."

"What happened?"

"You tell me." I indicated my dismay by exaggerating my investigation of the street. "I don't see another damaged vehicle around here."

"There isn't."

I pointed at my car. "That's a hell of a hit-and-run."

"Hmm. Yeah."

"Did I do something wrong? Was I parked illegally?"

"No. Let's see your driver's license."

I reached for my wallet. "I guess I need to get a tow truck out here."

"I've got one coming."

"Where's the fire department?"

"They'll be here in a couple of minutes."

I gave the officer my driver's license. "This is considered a hazmat incident these days."

The officer studied my driver's license. "How did you know that?"

"Here." I gave him my fire department's picture I.D.

"Ah, look at you—Norfolk Fire Department." He relaxed. "Now I know why you've been so at ease with me." He returned both I.D.s to me. "Well then, you know the drill. Sit tight."

"Right."

After an engine company from Baltimore's Fire Department arrived and secured the scene, they allowed me to get my travel bag out of the back seat of the car.

The police officer questioned me further to finish his report. The fire department captain questioned me for his report. And the tow truck operator questioned me about my insurance coverage, then informed his dispatcher.

I rode with the tow truck operator to the nearest Ford dealership. He waited for me to fill out the dealership's drop-off form.

After I completed the form, I placed it into their authorized manila envelope along with my car key, sealed the envelope, then slipped it through the dealership's night slot.

I climbed back into the tow truck. "Thanks for waiting."

"You're welcome. I'm headed back to the downtown area. You're welcome to come along."

"Thanks. Are there any decent hotels around there?"

"Sure. I'll be passing a few. Take your pick. No charge."

Once we were close to where my car had been wrecked, I chose a hotel. He took a hard right and drove into its parking lot.

"Thanks for the ride," I said, as he stopped the truck.

"No problem." He was ready for me to go. "I've got another call."

"I know. I heard it come in." I grabbed my travel bag. "Be safe." I stepped out of the truck's cab and watched him drive away.

I walked across the parking lot, entered the hotel's lobby, and searched for a pay telephone. I ignored the desk clerk's inquisitive expression.

I found a pay telephone in a hallway. It was mounted on a wall that separated the door to the MENS room from the door to the LADIES room. I called my insurance company and reported the accident, then I checked into the hotel at the front desk.

the lobby gave up its promise
and whispered, *this is second-best*;
the oily night clerk
had a single bed left

CHAPTER 18

His Idea of Poverty

Privileged. The Buddha came from the privileged class, Jansen. And still, today, he appeals to the privileged class. For The Buddha, poverty was a choice—it wasn't true poverty that he embraced. It was his idea of poverty, like Tolstoy's idea of poverty, which still meant that the necessities of food and clothing and shelter were always within reach. Always there—assumed, taken for granted. This is a small and controlled poverty.

Buddha's small poverty has not been noticed by those who have been privileged enough to adore and follow him. This small poverty has also been camouflaged by the privileged notion of spiritual poverty.

I know, Jansen. I know. The Buddha tried to liberate women and defied the caste system. Well, he had to get something right.

primitive feelings
in an empty bowl;
translating my hunger
into resurrected doubt

CHAPTER 19

What Was I Doing?

I slept badly. I rolled onto my right side and listened to the rain.

I sat up and swung my legs over the side of the bed—the bottoms of my feet tingled against the rough carpet. I took a deep breath, then shook my head as I exhaled.

What was I doing? The past that I was seeking in Baltimore had abandoned me. It only exists inside of myself. I can't touch it. I can't step into the presence. I can't—

I stood up and went to the window. The morning light forced me to squint when I pushed aside the curtain.

Rain continued to assault the city. Vehicles crawled through the flooded streets. A brave pedestrian leaned into the angle of the rain shielded by her black umbrella.

"Yeah. It's only a matter of time before you're alone again."

A piece of wisdom—no—a simple fact in my knowledge from somewhere in the past; can't remember where—here, somewhere. It doesn't matter. I realize that now. "Hmm. The past is no longer here."

The gray light of the morning. No longer squinting. The window.

the clouds unpinned themselves
from the diesel-exhausted sky;
watching the passing bus,
watching the syllables of rain

CHAPTER 20

I'm Cookie. Do You Remember Me?

I felt foolish. I took leave from work to come to Baltimore and look: here I am leaving already—end of quest.

I waited in the lounge area of the hotel's lobby for the car rental agency to deliver their vehicle to me after I checked out of my room.

The mid-sized lobby was plain and the smell of chemical solvents indicated their effort at keeping it reasonably clean. There were three small tables with chairs arranged near a counter that ran the length of the back wall of the lobby's lounge area. Upon the counter, there was a coffee maker with all the essentials for providing coffee to their guests: Styrofoam cups, coffee creamer, sugar, artificial sweetener, red plastic stirring sticks, and paper napkins.

I set my travel bag beside a chair at one of the small tables and approached the coffee maker. I liberated a Styrofoam cup from the stack of cups and poured myself some complimentary coffee. The coffee was hot and good.

I approached the main entrance of the lobby, as I continued drinking my coffee, to look outside. The automatic glass double doors opened, indicating that I had to step back to let them close again. I studied the street from the required distance after the doors closed.

Traffic, both pedestrian and vehicular, was heavy and intense. The rain had eased to a drizzle. I peered at the clock behind the front desk on my right and discovered that I was witnessing rush-hour traffic. The front desk clerk ignored me.

A Chevy Blazer pulled into the hotel's carport that sheltered the hotel's main entrance. The driver stepped out of the vehicle.

I squinted at him. I sipped my coffee. There was something familiar about him.

I went back to the lobby area and sat at my table.

The man entered the lobby, made a quick search of the interior, and saw me.

He squinted at me. He hesitated. He approached me. "Llewellen?"

I hesitated. "Yes?" I set my coffee cup on the table and stood up. I pointed at the vehicle parked underneath the carport. "Is . . . is that my rental vehicle?"

"Yes."

"Good."

"Are you ready to go?"

"Yes."

"I'll take you to the rental office so you can do the paperwork there."

"Great." I reached for my travel bag.

"Llewellen."

The tone of his familiar voice stopped me from grabbing the handle of my bag. I straightened up and looked at him more closely instead. "Do I know you?"

"Llewellen."

"That's my name, alright."

"Welcome back."

"Do I know you?" I repeated.

"I'm Cookie. Do you remember me?"

"Cookie. Of course. Yes. Jesus."

"No. Buddha."

"Yes." We shook hands as I added, "Jansen considered you a pessimist, a devout cynic, a man who saw a shadow in all things."

"That's me."

"Damn. How are you?"

"I don't know."

"Ah. Yes—I don't know."

"That was not an intentional Buddhist statement."

"Jansen considered you to be a Master."

"Jansen. Hmm. Jansen. I'm a Master, alright; master of downward mobility—from a short-order cook to a part-time driver for a car rental agency."

"Still—you knew Jansen."

Cookie raised his hands for emphasis. "I don't know."

I nodded. "Yes, of course. I don't know."

Cookie shrugged. "There you are—a very nice reflection."

"Of what?

"Of . . . of proper Zen, I suppose."

I frowned. "That's behind me now."

"Oh, yeah? Then why are you here?"

"Because . . . because . . . ."

"You really don't know."

"Well, I . . . I—yes."

"I see."

I pursed my lips in dismay.

"No false sense of humility."

I was not sure why I grinned.

"I could use a little coffee, Llew."

"Coffee—sure, of course." I grabbed my Styrofoam cup and escorted Cookie to the coffee counter. I liberated another Styrofoam cup from the stack and poured him a fresh cup. I replenished mine.

I shifted my travel bag to the other side of my chair and invited him to sit down at my table. We drank our coffee in silence for a while.

Cookie's beard was long and his shoulder-length hair was pulled back into a ponytail. His angular features were sharp, and his pallor appeared malnourished. His brown eyes lacked luster. He wore a pair of Army surplus boots, a pair of faded jeans, a blue sports jacket, and an orange cap with the logo HTZ embroidered in the front. He appeared to be much older than when I saw him last. He looked to be a man who might be approaching his sixties. I don't know why—

"You know," Cookie leaned against the table using both of his forearms for support, "a shot of rye would improve this coffee a whole lot."

"I have to admit, that would be a little too early for me."

Cookie was disappointed by my response. "I don't want to take any more of your time." He stood up. "Let me take you to the rental office and I'll be gone."

"Wait. Hold on there. Sit down. Drink your coffee."

He sat down.

"You're the reason why I'm here," I declared.

"Ah. Then you do know why you're here."

"Well."

"And I believe I forced you into humility."

"Not forced."

"Right." Cookie pressed his back against the chair. "So. Nothing is behind you."

"I . . . I guess you're right."

"And?"

"You. You're the past I was looking for in Baltimore."

"The past in the present." Cookie smirked. "I see."

"Or is it the other way around?"

"You poor bastard."

"What?"

"Didn't Jansen teach you anything?"

"Sometimes I'm not sure."

Cookie nodded. "That's an honest answer."

I shrugged. "So. So—what have you been doing since Jansen's death?"

"Nothing."

"Well. This job you have—that's something."

"That's temporary. Part time. That's nothing."

"I see."

"Don't see."

"That's what Jansen would have said."

"I'm not Jansen."

I sipped my coffee. "Where do you live?"

"Here. I mean, you know, Baltimore."

"And?"

"And . . . and I was married to a decent woman who, well—she finally got impatient with me."

"Oh?"

"She kicked me out of our place."

"Ah."

"It's alright." Cookie grimaced. "Women."

"What?"

"They're difficult."

"Yeah."

"They're always asking questions. You know? They always want answers."

"Mine wanted new furniture," I said.

"You're lucky."

"She left me. Recently."

"Damn. You, too."

"Yeah."

"Wife?"

"No."

"I see." Cookie stared at his coffee. "At least you don't have a room full of furniture to worry about— new or old."

"Yeah. Well."

"I can sure use a drink," he declared.

"I'll buy."

"I don't need charity."

"You looked out for me and Jansen."

"Yeah, well—that didn't save your souls."

"They couldn't be saved," I said.

Cookie frowned with approval. "Llew, my boy, I almost believe Jansen might have learned you something."

"Cute. You know, a smile would have softened that remark."

"I don't feel like smiling."

"You used to smile."

"Yeah, well—I used to listen to classical music. I used to have a soul."

"Fish is dead," I said.

"Oh. I didn't know that."

"Cancer."

"Rotten way to go. Largo and Zack are—"

"Dead. I know. Both murdered. No apparent reasons."

"Rotten way to go." Cookie shook his head. "There you have it."

"Yeah."

"I miss Jansen."

"Me too," I whispered.

"Also killed for no apparent reason."

"For no *good* reason," I clarified. "Rotten way to go."

"All dead," Cookie muttered. "You don't live that kind of life without a lot of risks."

"Yeah."

Cookie stretched. "So, do you still want this vehicle?"

"No. I want you to have a drink instead."

"Now you're talking." Cookie stood up.

"And I've decided to stay here."

"Good. I'll return the vehicle."

"I'll go with you. Wait here a minute. Have another cup of coffee."

"I need to use the telephone," he said.

"Sure. Fine."

I checked back into the hotel and I got a room with two beds.

Cookie called the car rental agency using the front desk's telephone to inform them of the cancellation.

I went upstairs to my new room and dropped off my travel bag.

Cookie drove us to the car rental office where I officially canceled the reservation and where he officially quit his job. As soon as we walked out of the rental agency, I suggested that we have that drink. He recommended a place, then led the way.

It was no longer raining. It was a short walk.

a plague of penniless drunks
in a rue of devotion
boiled into the sidewalk
from Harry's Bar & Grill

CHAPTER 21

Jansen is Dead

As soon as we sat at the corner of the L-shaped bar, the bartender served each of us a shot of rye and a long neck bottle of beer.

I was perplexed.

Cookie noticed my expression. "I'm a regular here." He picked up his shot glass. "He figured you'd want what I was having."

"I see." I placed a twenty-dollar bill on the bar.

Cookie tossed down his rye. He shivered with relief before he set the empty shot glass on the bar. "Damn, I needed that. Damn."

I tossed down my shot. I exhaled. I nodded. "Yeah."

We drank our beer in silence.

The bartender took the twenty.

We finished our beer.

The bartender served us another round of drinks and placed my change on the bar.

I picked up my shot glass and studied the amber liquid it contained. "How long has it been?"

"I don't know." Cookie scooped up his shot glass, tossed down the rye then gently set the glass on the bar. "Drink up."

"Right." My second shot did not burn. "Do you still practice? Do you meditate?"

Cookie peered at me after he drank half his bottle of beer. "You mean—zazen?"

"Yes. Of course. Sitting—zazen."

"Look. I don't sit. I don't meditate." He hesitated as if he needed a moment to gather enough patience to address me. "Zen is dead. God is dead. I'm a bad guy. I started out that way and, well, I guess that's my way. Jansen never judged."

"I'm not—"

"Jansen—never messed with my head."

"I'm not—"

"Jansen—is dead."

"Alright." I grabbed my bottle of beer and drank deeply.

Cookie finished his beer, then placed the empty bottle on the bar. "Sorry. I'm not buzzed yet."

"Me neither."

He grinned. I laughed. We shot another rye and drank more beer. We got buzzed.

Jansen's broken arpeggios,
an ancient set and drift;
wading through the stream
of his crimson past

CHAPTER 22

He Smelled Bad

Baltimore's past had finally presented itself to me. But I wasn't sure that I was going to like where this past was taking me.

The beer and rye had taken effect. Cookie's intense need to drink was infectious.

When we left the tavern, we walked unsteadily along a street that was littered with trash and broken glass.

"Where are we going?" I asked.

"I don't know," Cookie answered.

I pulled my jacket's zipper up to my throat as if that was going to protect me from the unknown. I tried to understand what I was doing here and now and then, suddenly, a disheveled character approached me at a street corner.

He smelled bad. He looked ill. The bitter end of a cigarette butt smoldered from the right corner of his mouth.

He grabbed the right lapel of his threadbare jacket and with an accompanied glance upward he indicated the sky with his left hand.

He suppressed a cough. He did not speak.

consumptive mime
begs for a handout;
he flicks away his spent cigarette
as he accepts my three singles

CHAPTER 23

Tramping

Cookie took me to another tavern where we drank a couple of beers and exchanged friendly talk with the inhabitants, then we left.

We stayed on the move. We traveled without purpose. More rye and more beer intensified our purposelessness.

I did not notice when I forgot myself among the lost souls in the taverns and on the streets. I did not remember at what point I disappeared and became at one with—what?

Nausea.

I vomited in an alley. Cookie watched without emotion, waited without concern.

Drifting.

I saw myself leaning against an alley wall.

Tramping.

I stepped over discarded bottles and vagabonds on the pavement, and—I stepped into a pathetic realization: this was not Zen.

radiant whispers
from sidewalk vagrants;
rough comments,
deranged perspectives

CHAPTER 24

I Need a Drink

I woke up in response to a chink of light that burned through a crack caused by a small separation between the window curtains.

I tried to sit up but my head hurt too much. I closed my eyes and rolled onto my side instead. I opened my eyes and recognized my hotel room. Cookie was lying in the other bed.

"How did I get here?" I muttered. Cookie didn't answer. "How did we get here?"

"I followed you," Cookie mumbled.

"You *did*?"

He rubbed his eyelids. "You took care of your clothes and everything." He rolled onto his side toward me, then pointed to my blue jeans and shirt that were draped over the back of a chair. "See?"

"I did that?"

"Well, I certainly didn't."

"Damn. And you?"

"Me? What? Oh." Cookie cleared his throat. "I'm not that fastidious. I slept in my clothes." He raised his left leg. "See?" He lowered his leg, then exhaled as if that small physical effort had taken all the strength he had available in his body.

I sighed. "I've got a terrible headache."

"Me, too."

"Man."

"I need a drink."

I looked at the clock. "At this hour?"

"What hour is that?"

I massaged my temples. "Right. You would say that. What was I thinking?" I swung my legs over the side of the bed and sat up. "Whoa." I leaned forward and supported my upper body by placing the back of my forearm against the tops of my thighs. "Damn." My hands were ink-stained. "Where did we go last night? What did we do?"

"Don't ask me. I was there, remember?"

I stood up, steadied myself, and went into the bathroom. I leaned against the sink and opened the spigot.

hands in hot water,
stained with blue-black tattoos;
the unworthy newsprint-past
washed down the bathroom sink

CHAPTER 25

Mother of God

I sighed when I saw the empty coffee pot in the lobby.

"Forget the coffee," Cookie said, as we shambled across the lobby, through the main entrance, and onto the sidewalk. "This way." He guided me to a tavern. "I know the hours and location to every joint in town."

When we reached the establishment, he pulled open the door. "It's not much to look at inside, but they pour generous drinks."

Cookie ordered a screwdriver—vodka and orange juice—after he sat on a bar stool. I ordered coffee, then climbed onto the stool beside him.

The bartender placed two cardboard coasters on the bar before he served us.

"What are you doing, Cookie?"

"What do you mean?"

I sipped my black coffee, which made me feel better. I ignored Cookie's sullen demeanor. I stared at my coffee. "Are you alright?"

"No."

"Another drink won't help"

"I know. But I'll have one, anyway."

I nodded at the bartender.

Cookie grew more somber.

"Everybody wants to be somebody." Cookie plucked an ice cube from his glass and ate it. "But in the end, we become nobody." He wiped his mouth with the back of his left hand. "Nobody."

We left the tavern and walked without talking for a long time. The fresh air felt good and clean.

Cookie placed his right hand on my shoulder and drew my attention to the church that we were approaching on our left. "Do you go to church?"

"No." I followed him to the main entrance.

He began to reach for one of the door handles, then decided not to. He turned abruptly to me instead. "Why?"

I came to a halt. "I don't know."

Cookie turned away from me, pulled open the door, and invited me to accompany him. Once inside, he made the Sign of the Cross—he was Catholic. We were alone.

I relaxed. I always found the interior silence of an empty Catholic Church to be calming.

I liked seeing the Stations of the Cross, depicting the Passion of Christ from his condemnation to his burial, posted on the walls—seven on each side of the church.

I liked the interior's spiritual darkness—cool and musty. And because this was an old church that had been built before the influence of the Vatican Council II upon the 1960s, there was still a kneeling rail that ran the width of the church several feet in front of the altar.

Cookie knelt before Mother of God 's statue and again graced himself with the Sign of the Cross. A bank of votive candles flickered at her feet.

I saw a wounded conscience, a lost soul, a man whose future was in question. And, perhaps, in all that, I saw these elements in myself as well.

I knelt upon the small kneeling rail beside him, pressed the palms of my hands together, and thought about why I was here. When I peered at Cookie, I saw tears streaming down his face. I was alarmed by the seriousness of those tears.

"Forgive me," Cookie muttered to Holy Mother. "Please. Forgive me."

I clenched my hands into a double fist, but I did not pretend to pray. I pressed my forearms against the kneeling rail that was constructed in front of the bank of votive candles that flickered by the grace and by the monetary donations of previous believers. The representative light of these tiny souls fortified my courage. "Are you alright?"

"No."

"Is there anything I can do to help?"

"I am lost—forever. Doomed. Hell-bound." He shifted uneasily on his knees. "Nothing and no one can help me."

I bit my lower lip.

Cookie bowed his head and pressed his forehead against his clenched hands. "I needed God yesterday. But God was not present." Cookie unclenched his hands and looked up at Holy Mother. He shook his head. "Where is God?"

I searched for a response. "They say that we . . . we can hear God through our souls."

"What the hell does that mean?"

"I don't know, I . . . I—"

"And who the hell is *they*?"

I shrugged.

"Has your soul ever heard God?"

"I was trying to help you."

"Fine. Okay." Cookie's irritation flattened. "What good is God, Llew?"

I didn't know.

"I'll tell you—no good at all."

"Then why pray to God's mother?"

"I like mothers. I trust them. They have strength. They give us life." Cookie bowed his head. "But she's nothing, too. I know that. She's a lie. I'm still fooling myself. I know that. It's a habit. But I do know that I come from a mother. I don't know that I come from God." Cookie gazed at the image of Mary's angelic figure. "It's no good."

I straightened my back and shifted away from Cookie to distribute my weight more evenly upon my knees.

Cookie bowed his head before Holy Mother and graced himself with the Sign of the Cross. "In the name of the Father, and of the Son, and of the Holy Ghost, Amen." The bank of flickering votive candles illuminated Holy Mother's feet.

> that strange ache of faith
> offered its crude illumination
> upon two brittle
> terra cotta souls

CHAPTER 26

Outside Ourselves

The side street tavern we had entered was occupied with serious drinkers. The place felt safe and remote and shut off from the sounds of outdoor urban activity.

Silence.

We stood at the bar for a long time. The surface of my coffee reflected the tavern's overhead light.

Cookie grabbed his glass and tossed down the shot of rye.

"You need to go easy on that."

"Says you."

He wanted to order two doubles on the rocks.

"I'm not paying for that."

Cookie ignored me.

"Let's sit at one of those booths."

Cookie glanced at the three unoccupied booths that were arranged against the wall parallel to the bar.

I picked up my mug of coffee. "Come on. It'll be more comfortable over there." I chose the corner booth and sat down.

Cookie joined me after he finished his drink. It appeared as if he were struggling to say something but couldn't find the right words. "I need another drink."

I shrugged. "No."

He waved at the bartender. When he caught his attention, he presented the back of his left hand and displayed his first and second fingers.

The bartender nodded with understanding.

"Drinks are on their way."

"I've had enough."

"Whatever." He placed his left elbow on the table, raised his forearm, and cradled his forehead upon the palm of his left hand. He closed his eyes and waited for his next drink.

I studied Cookie.

Even after making allowances for all this drinking, he appeared dangerously disjointed and disturbed about something—something, perhaps, other than his failed marriage and his loss of faith. Admittedly, this would be enough for anybody to look and to act badly. But for some reason, I felt there was something more.

I pursed my lips to prevent myself from speaking.

Cookie had never been truly one of us—that is, he was never a member of that ragged and homeless street group of mendicants from the past: Zack and Largo, Fish and Jansen and me. It appeared that Cookie had kept both feet on the ground and his mind in the real world during those days so many years ago. He was married and had a steady job at the burger joint and, well, it appeared as if he was centered and clear. Jansen respected the depth of his Zen Buddhist practice and his spiritual independence.

So what was it? There was something more; that one more something that had become . . . become too much to live with.

The bartender set two drinks on the table and took the twenty-dollar bill that Cookie presented to him.

"So, you do have money," I said.

"Emergency money."

I pushed aside the drink intended for me. "I see."

Cookie stared past me. "Don't see."

The bartender placed the change from the twenty on the table.

Cookie reached for one of the drinks as soon as the bartender left.

outside ourselves
reaching for faith;
outside our minds,
reaching for peace

CHAPTER 27

This is Not a Crime

City twilight greeted us when we stepped out of the tavern's artificial darkness.

"I need to get something to eat," I declared. "I'm starving and—" I realized that Cookie was no longer beside me. He had disappeared. "What the heck—?"

I stopped walking and turned around. A police car slowed down as it approached me. When I waved at the officer, he nodded then accelerated past me. As soon as the squad car turned right at the street corner, Cookie emerged from a nearby alley. "What are you doing?"

"Cops."

"So?"

"I don't trust them."

"We're not doing anything wrong."

Cookie approached me. "Just being in this part of town is doing something wrong."

"I don't remember that when I was—"

"Whatever."

"Okay. Whatever." I was a little annoyed by his dismissal. "Well. Anyway. I'm hungry, damn it."

"I know a cheap Italian place." Cookie started walking. "They serve good food."

"Lead on." I followed him.

The Italian restaurant was located in a strip mall. It was small and clean and inexpensive. We sat at one of the tables against the wall. The place was half-full with neighborhood diners. I ordered spaghetti and meatballs for both of us; he asked for a carafe of skull busting burgundy.

The waitress was nice and efficient. She was quick about serving us the wine with a basket of bread. She poured wine into our glasses and asked us what dressing we wanted with the small salad that came with the spaghetti dinner. I ordered the house dressing. Cookie indicated the same with a nod. The salads arrived after I consumed two slices of garlic bread. The salad was fresh.

"You need to eat, Cookie."

Cookie stabbed a tomato wedge with his fork then ate it.

The waitress served us large bowls of spaghetti in a marinara sauce topped with two large meatballs.

We ate in silence. The food was good.

Cookie finished eating first and pushed aside his bowl of half-eaten spaghetti. It appeared as if he wanted to say something but he didn't.

"Are you alright?" I asked.

He drank the rest of his wine. He scowled as if he had drunk poison, then set the glass on the table. "Where are we going? What are we doing?"

I pushed aside my empty bowl. "You're asking the wrong person." I picked up my wine glass by its stem. "Where is anybody going?" I drank the rest of my wine and set the empty glass on the table.

The waitress approached us before Cookie was able to respond to my hypothetical question. "Can I interest either of you in dessert?"

"No, thank you," I said.

Cookie simply shook his head.

"More wine?"

"Just the check," I answered.

"Alright." She smiled. "You don't have to hurry out. Please, take your time."

"Thank you."

Cookie poured what was left in the carafe into our glasses. "Why are you hanging around with me?"

"I told you that you're—"

"Why? Why do you seem to care about me?"

"Because you're . . . you're Cookie. And you—"

"Owe me nothing."

"But you fed me and Jansen and Fish and—"

"I was wrong," Cookie announced. "Jansen taught you nothing."

I felt helpless. "Alright. Alright."

The waitress returned with the check. I paid the bill and gave her a generous tip.

She smiled. "Thank you." Then she left us alone.

I stared at my wine.

"I'm lost forever," he declared.

"All of us are lost," I said.

"I told you in church. I don't believe anymore."

"In what?" I prompted.

"I don't believe—"

"In . . . ."

"God—damn it."

We stared.

"Disbelief in God is not a crime."

"I know that!"

"Easy, Cookie." I glanced at a couple of nearby tables and smiled apologetically at those who were disturbed by Cookie's outburst. "People will think you're crazy."

He leaned toward me and whispered. "I *am* crazy, man. We went to church together, remember?" He straightened up, then leaned against the wall beside our table. "I told you, you owe me nothing. You can go now."

"I'm not going anywhere."

He sulked. "I killed her, Llew."

I grabbed my glass of wine in response. I spilled some of the wine. "Metaphorically speaking, right?"

"Yeah, yeah—you know what I meant."

I wiped the spilled wine off the table with my paper napkin. "A lot of guys have done that."

Cookie blinked hard. "It's over."

"No, it's not."

Cookie inhaled deeply, then exhaled. "The truth is—my wife can't stand the sight of me anymore."

"But—"

"It's over."

"Cookie."

I bit my lower lip. I did not know what to say. I peered at a table across the room where two women sat drinking wine while waiting for their dinner. Like us, they were talking furtively, and intensely. The lady facing me was a matronly brunette. She was aware of our presence. She was aware that I was scrutinizing her. She was aware that we might be dangerous.

her nervous laughter,
a thin arabesque;
her red lipstick,
a painted gash

CHAPTER 28

Nobody Knows Anybody

The night we encountered after leaving the restaurant felt cold.

I walked alongside Cookie for awhile then suddenly found myself following him into a dark alley. "Where are we going?"

Cookie answered my question when we reached its dead end. "This is where I leave you, Llew." He reached into the left inside pocket of his blue sports jacket and pulled out a .38 snub-nosed revolver.

I was so startled by the revolver's appearance that I took an involuntary step backward. "Take it easy, Cookie."

"You don't know Jansen."

"I . . . I don't know him—sure . . . sure, you're right."

Cookie smirked. "You don't know me."

"I can try."

"Nobody knows anybody."

"I . . . I . . . ."

"You don't even know yourself," he muttered with contempt.

"That's not true."

"Then what are you doing in Baltimore if it's not about trying to find yourself?"

"I . . . I . . . ."

"Right. And nobody knows anybody. We are all miserable—and alone." Cookie placed the revolver's muzzle against his right temple.

"Don't!" I reached for the revolver.

Cookie raised his left arm then straightened it toward me to block my advance. "I meant what I said. I've come to the end of myself."

"Cookie, don't!" I pushed his left arm aside and grabbed his right forearm as he squeezed the trigger.

I released his forearm and I crouched simultaneously in response to the plosive report of the revolver. Cookie fell to the ground—the revolver clattered when it hit the pavement.

I knelt beside him. "Cookie."

Blood oozed from his head wound.

I touched his carotid artery. There was a pulse.

I studied his injury. The bullet did not appear to have penetrated his skull. My attempt to deflect his aim had been successful. However, his scalp was deeply grazed by the bullet and . . . and he was traumatized, unconscious, and in need of medical attention.

I searched Cookie and found a leather wallet in the right rear pocket of his trousers. I opened it, reached inside the billfold, and found his Maryland driver's license. I had trouble reading his name in the badly lit alley. "Charles Patrick Anderson. Hmm. So that's who you are—whoever you are."

He lived in Baltimore. I memorized his address. "Okay. Okay."

I slipped the driver's license into the wallet, then shoved the wallet into his back pocket.

"Charles Patrick Anderson. You idiot." I glanced at the alley's entrance to see if anybody was there. Apparently, nobody heard the shot.

I stood up and peered at the narrow sky. I felt empty.

bare branches of penance,
living by small clues;
this habit of prayer,
a worthless endowment

CHAPTER 29

Under a Small Sky

I approached the entrance of the alley.

Still. Nobody.

I stepped out of the alley and onto the sidewalk, then crossed the street.

"There's no reward in the end," I muttered to myself as I walked and I walked to find a pay telephone so that I could call for an ambulance.

This was not what I had expected to discover in Baltimore.

under a small sky,
feeling a broken breeze;
discovering
the border of emptiness

CHAPTER 30

Charles Patrick Anderson

I made the 911 emergency-call from a pay telephone that was attached to the exterior wall of a busy convenience store. I presented my back to the parking lot; I cupped my left hand over my mouth and over the telephone's receiver.

I reported that I saw an unconscious man lying in an alley. I reported that he appeared to be bleeding.

I did not tell the dispatcher that I knew this man because I did not know this . . . this Charles Patrick Anderson.

I did not give the dispatcher my name; I gave him the street address nearest the alley, instead, before I hung up the telephone.

I heard my deposited coin drop into the telephone's change return. I reached inside the return and fished out my quarter.

Was that the best I could do?

I felt disappointed with myself.

Why did I find it necessary to conceal my identity when I reported that Cookie was lying in an alley? Why couldn't I commit myself to . . . to . . . .

I did not know Charles Patrick Anderson. Nice justification.

I tapped the top of the pay telephone with the heel of my left hand.

> half-measures, intensifying
> my four-point ellipsis;
> this grave disappointment
> strips me of my shadow

CHAPTER 31

With Empty Pockets

I sauntered back to the alley in an effort to appear carefree. I ignored the blare of the ambulance that rushed past me as well as the lights and siren of a police car that followed shortly after. By the time I arrived at the scene, there was a small crowd of people standing near the alley's entrance where the ambulance and the police car were parked. I joined the crowd and watched the paramedics package the man, who I continued to think of as Cookie, onto a stretcher.

As they transported him out of the alley and into the ambulance, I heard one of the paramedics say to the police officer that they were taking Cookie to Johns Hopkins Hospital.

He was still alive and he was receiving medical attention. For now, that's all I needed to know.

I was exhausted. Depressed.

I needed to get some rest. I needed to shut down for a while.

staggering away
with empty pockets,
within empty circles
of unknowing

CHAPTER 32

Adolescent Enlightenment

The Four Noble Truths have no meaning—have no truth; there will always be suffering in this world. And the Eightfold Path is not the solution to end suffering—to end anything.

The divine does not reveal itself in the world.

adolescent enlightenment
born from privilege;
absolute insights
presenting relative solutions

CHAPTER 33

Quest for Tranquility

I did not turn on the lights when I entered my hotel room. I left the *Do Not Disturb* sign hanging on the room's outer door latch.

Cookie's unmade bed taunted my quest for tranquility.

I sat on the upholstered chair that was placed in the corner of the room on the left side of the window. I kicked off my shoes and propped my feet upon my unmade bed and stared into the darkness.

What happened? What now?

heartbreaking
life and death;
nature's struggle
makes no sense

CHAPTER 34

Catherine, My Wife

My neck cracked when I shifted into another slouched position in search of comfort—sleeplessness felt worse in bed.

My disdain for the approach of daybreak intensified as the night hours deepened.

I rose from the upholstered chair and drew the window curtains more tightly together to prevent any crust of light from entering my hotel room.

I returned to the chair. I pressed my head against the back of it—my neck ached. I blinked.

Silence and darkness and the illusion that the outside world had come to a stop permitted me to address my clumsy thoughts.

What happened between Cookie and his wife? What happened between me and Sandy? What happened to my memory of Catherine, my deceased wife—the person who had brought love and value to my life. Even now, the pain of her loss left me feeling hollow and gray.

Black was nothing. Gray was something. The night brought the comfort of blackness—no color. The day brought the discomfort of gray—the threat of color.

pasting a conjunctive expression
upon a gray and empty space;
blackened thoughts,
broken glass

CHAPTER 35

Robert Llewellen

I woke up feeling terrible.

I had finally fallen asleep in the upholstered chair. My sleep had been fitful.

I shifted in my chair until I attained some measure of comfort, then gazed into the stillness of the room's darkness.

I drifted. I closed my eyes. "Cookie." I opened my eyes as I sat up. "Who is Cookie?"

I stood up. I needed to go to the hospital. "Who is Charles Patrick Anderson?"

I shook my head in a silly attempt to clear my head. "Who am I?" I unbuttoned my shirt. "You're an idiot, Robert Llewellen."

I decided to take a shower and change my clothes before I launched into an investigation that was tangential to the one I had planned to conduct while in Baltimore.

I decided to take a long shower.

deaf from chanting
about lost incarnations;
bruised from dancing
with character defects

CHAPTER 36

That Dreadful Word

I walked to John Hopkins Hospital after having a light breakfast of coffee and toast at a diner.

I entered the hospital's main lobby and approached a lady who sat behind the visitors' information counter. I waited for us to make eye contact. "Charles Anderson. He's a patient here."

"Anderson." She repeated. "One moment, please."

"Sure. Sure." I leaned against the counter with my back to her to indicate that I was in no hurry.

I wanted to appear casual. I wanted to disguise my sudden concern over the possibility of police presence because of Cookie's attempted suicide. I relaxed.

everything has a word
connected to a meaning;
getting there from here,
everywhere is somewhere

CHAPTER 37

Don't See So Clearly

The elevator took me to the third floor. When the elevator's door opened, I saw a sign with two arrows pointing in opposite directions: each was associated with a series of room numbers. The arrow pointing to my left, which corresponded with a set of decreasing numbers, included Cookie's room. The elevator's door closed as soon as I stepped onto the hallway and veered left.

As I walked along the hallway, where the odd-numbered rooms were on my left and the even-numbered rooms were on my right, I saw sick men and women on beds and on chairs—each of their illnesses tried to represent themselves at a glance. All doors were open, including the one leading into Cookie's room.

I approached the even-numbered threshold with caution. My silence intensified when I saw a trim-figured woman sitting in a chair by his bed. I was confused by her presence and by her declared intimacy.

She looked at me after sensing my presence. "Hello."

"Hi."

She was an attractive woman. Her short black hair framed her delicate facial features; her cobalt blue eyes shined despite her obvious emotional distress. She wore a brown jacket over a beige blouse that was tucked inside a plain black skirt.

I stepped into the room. "I . . . I came here to see how Cookie was doing."

She pursed her lips, then studied me with sudden interest. "Charles is going to be alright."

"I . . . I see. Good."

"Are . . . are you a friend?"

"Yes. I'm a friend. And . . . and you are . . . ."

"His wife, Teresa."

"Oh."

She stood up in response to my embarrassment. "And you are . . . ."

"Llewellen. Robert Llewellen. But everybody calls me Llew."

"Ahh." Sudden recognition and interest brightened her beauty. "Llewellen. Cookie. Yes. Names from the past."

I nodded. "Yeah." I bit my lower lip.

"You were associated with Jansen, weren't you?"

"Weren't we all?"

She nodded. "Yes. Jansen. That Jansen. And you. I remember hearing about you."

"I see. Well . . . ."

She looked at Cookie. "Do you know anything about this?"

"No. I don't."

"Then how did you know he was here?"

"I prevented him from killing himself."

"You. So, you are involved."

"A little. But that doesn't mean I know anything about this."

"I see."

"Please—don't see so clearly."

She frowned. "I've given up trying."

I did not know how to respond to that.

She sat down. "Thank you."

"For what?"

"You said that you prevented—"

"Forget it."

She looked at Cookie. She was close to tears.

"Don't cry. Please."

"I'm a woman. What's left?"

"I see."

"Don't see so clearly."

I pursed my lips. "I deserved that." I approached Cookie. "Asleep?"

"Yes," she said.

Cookie's head was wrapped in a bandage. It looked as if his shoulder-length ponytail had been cut off. In fact, judging by the thickness of his head wrap, it appeared as if his head might have been shaved. His long and unruly beard had been severely trimmed as well. He looked old and worn out—spent.

A clear plastic tube was wrapped around his placid face. The tube had two small plastic prongs that were inserted into his nostrils—a cannula. It provided him with the oxygen to help him breathe, but not with the desire to help him live. There was an I.V. syringe stuck into his right forearm that was attached to a plastic tube that allowed clear fluid to flow from a plastic bag into his unconscious veins— saline solution.

"Why did he do it?" she whispered.

"You're asking *me*?"

"You knew him."

"*You're* his wife."

"You were with him last. On a drunk."

"We had a few drinks."

"It's never a few drinks."

"Well." I exhaled in an effort to control my bewilderment. "I understand."

"Thank you."

"Can I get you anything?" I whispered. "Coffee? A soda?"

She did not answer.

"Where are you staying?" I asked.

She squinted at me. "Staying?"

"I—that is—Cookie said something about a breakup between—" I shrugged my shoulders—"You know."

"I'm still at home."

"Did you kick him out?"

"He wouldn't quit drinking."

"Okay."

"He couldn't."

"Right."

"I had to," she whispered.

"Yes."

"I had to throw him out."

"He probably knew that," I said.

"We left each other—over time."

"He told me he killed you."

She nodded. "He . . . he was killing me." She bowed her head. "I cannot save him."

She suddenly seemed older.

I left without saying goodbye.

her makeup
was not abstract;
her eyes
were not blue

CHAPTER 38

Who Was Teresa?

I stepped out of the elevator into the hospital's main lobby.

Who was Teresa?

I hunted for the cafeteria until I found it.

Whoever she was, I liked her.

I bought coffee, then sat at an unoccupied table near a window. I placed the coffee on the table and stared at the heated vapors that rose out of the Styrofoam cup.

She seemed like . . . like Sandy. She seemed practical—aware of her impasse with Cookie.

I stretched my back and took a deep breath.

Had Sandy and I left each other over time as well?

I shook my head.

Well, I wasn't killing her.

The hot black coffee burned my tongue. "Damn."

reaching in all directions:
the four corners of nowhere;
the ten thousand things are
just one more illusion

CHAPTER 39

Nobody Answering

I found a pay telephone in the hospital's ground floor lobby.

I reached into my left trouser pocket and found enough change for a three-minute long distance call.

I deposited the money and dialed Sandy's mother. I knew that's where Sandy would be staying.

Message machine announcement. Nobody home. Nobody answering.

I waited for the beep.

"Hi, Sandy. I . . . I was thinking about you and . . . and I hope you're alright." I suddenly didn't know what else to say. "Love you. Bye."

I hung up the telephone and listened to my change drop into the telephone's coin box.

I left the hospital and wandered the streets of Baltimore and tried to disappear by escaping into life in the way I thought I had been able to do so many years ago when I was lost and homeless and with Jansen. And when I failed to disappear, I realized that those so-called disappearances were into Jansen's life—not mine.

If Jansen were still alive, he would not have told me that I was a failure even though I was still trying too hard to escape into . . . into—yes, if Jansen were still alive.

I returned to the hospital.

Teresa was gone.

I sat in the green plastic chair by Cookie's bed. I gazed at him through the stainless steel bed rails.

the train
had derailed;
the trip
had gone wrong

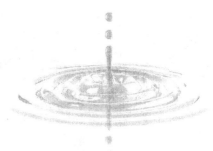

CHAPTER 40

Careful Pantomime

I knocked on the door of the third row-house from the corner. I turned away from the door and looked out upon the street as I waited on the porch for her to answer.

The one-way street was lined with parked cars on both sides. There was just enough clearance for a slow-moving vehicle to drive through this neighborhood's single lane.

I turned around as soon as I heard the turn of the latch and the scrape of the door opening.

Teresa appeared still dressed in what she had worn at the hospital. "Hello."

"I hope you don't mind."

"Come in." She stepped aside and, with the gesture of her left hand, invited me inside.

I walked into her dark living room and waited for her to close the door.

Her next gesture encouraged me to sit down on the sofa.

She hesitated near a stand-up lamp as she approached a chair that was arranged at a ninety-degree angle to the sofa; she did not turn on the light. She sat down and crossed her legs and did not engage me in conversation.

I leaned against the right arm of the sofa. She rested her hands on her lap.

careful pantomime
between strangers;
the darkness,
the welcomed silence

CHAPTER 41

Saints Confuse Me

"Jansen was not a saint," she said.

"Saints confuse me." I shifted away from the sofa's right arm.

"That was an observation derived from the past."

I looked down at the floor. "Observations don't always make the facts clear. They don't always lead to the truth."

"That leaves a lot of room to maneuver."

I nodded.

"Men. You're always seeking room to maneuver."

"The world is not black and white," I said.

"Listen to yourself." She chuckled cynically. "You think Jansen told you the truth."

"No. I didn't say he spoke the truth. He spoke about how he felt the truth was to him—not the truth itself. No." I shook my head. "That would have been a lie."

"You think you know something, Robert Llewellen."

Her contempt dissolved whatever degree of certainty I thought I had about the truth.

"Jansen spoke the truth."

"For heaven's sake, speak for yourself."

"Whoever that is."

"Christ." She uncrossed her legs. "Do you always run for cover?"

"Alright," I conceded. She sounded like Sandy talking about old furniture. "Alright."

She nodded.

The light from the street lamp peeked through a slit in the living room's window curtain.

She rose from her chair. "Would you like some coffee?"

"Sure."

"Come on."

I followed her into the kitchen.

treacherous whispers
about right and wrong;
the vanity of confession,
the impotence of truth

CHAPTER 42

Vietnam

"What's wrong with Cookie?" I asked.

Teresa handed me a cup of black coffee. No sugar. No answer.

I sat down at the kitchen table. She waited for me to drink some of my coffee.

I drank. "Good coffee." I placed my cup on the table.

She poured herself a cup and set the pot back onto the coffeemaker's warmer. "Something to do with the war."

"The War."

She sat down at the small kitchen table opposite me. "Vietnam."

"Of course."

She sipped her coffee then placed her cup on the table. "He lost something in that war or . . . or did something that he felt was wrong."

I sipped my coffee. "Are you alright?"
She shook her head. "I can't take it anymore."
She sipped her coffee.

the body language
of darkness,
another landscape
of distress

CHAPTER 43

Nothing Lasts

We believe. We suffer. And we need to believe because we suffer and don't know if there is truth in any belief.

A frightening thought this . . . this possibility that the narrow scope of existential philosophy might be close to approaching the truth: that nothing matters; that nothing lasts; that there is an end to all things; that life is absurd and meaningless; and that the universe has no rational direction or design. Truth is subjectivity, truth is a mere projection of thought, and truth is both an internal and external conception.

Perhaps this too is a lie.

existence
and God;
the holy communion,
the sacred absurdity

CHAPTER 44

Tough Woman

I had left Teresa without offering her any reassurance about Cookie. I believe she would have not drawn comfort from anything I would have had to say about the War— no matter how sincerely delivered.

As I walked back to my hotel, I thought about my Catherine. I detached myself from the surrounding noise of the street traffic. I felt her presence increase.

> in our world of worldly things:
> if detachment could be measured
> I would be the standard of weight
> on the other side of the scale

Several cars honked their horns at me as I jaywalked across the street. I smiled and waved at them.

Catherine often reminded me that I was too serious with myself. Occasionally, she was able to direct me away from my restlessness and guide me toward interludes of peace. Catherine felt present.

> tipped all the way to the table
> would be the standard's result, where
> the love for my wife would show, as
> my great vulnerability

CHAPTER 45

Lost in Uncertainty

I entered a familiar tavern—one that Cookie and I had visited during our drinking binge. I sat at the bar and ordered a club soda.

Two men were sitting at the bar. They were deeply involved in their own thoughts.

The bartender served me a glass of club soda with crushed ice and a twist of lemon.

I thanked him.

He nodded.

I slid my glass closer to me. I stared at the soda.

I thought about this . . . this spiritual quest that had . . . had become this . . . this what?

I drank my soda.

I thought about my spiritual—no—about the old, and then the new—furniture.

I bowed my head.

Catherine crowded my memory. Then there was
Sandy.

lost in uncertainty,
empty is not a feeling;
love is a sad endeavor,
between old and new furniture

CHAPTER 46

Combat Veteran

I thought a lot about the war as I walked back to my hotel. The War always crept into my mind without invitation.

Vietnam.

The sounds of small arms fire in the background of my mind intensified in pitch and frequency.

Post-war.

Jansen had been a true combat veteran; the sounds had been in him as well.

Beyond words.

Jansen had revealed his knowledge of those sounds to me only twice: different nights, only us, and never more. Our sounds twice shared in trust had been enough.

poor Vietnam,
a casualty
of time, almost
a relief

CHAPTER 47

Zen Noir

I visited Teresa the following morning after breakfast.

I waited a long time after knocking on her door.

She opened the front door of her row-house. She leaned against the doorjamb. "I wasn't going to answer the door."

"I'm glad you did."

She stepped aside. "Come in."

She closed the door after I stepped inside. She turned away from me and walked into the living room.

I followed her.

She indicated the sofa. "Make yourself comfortable. I have coffee."

"That would be nice. Black."

She nodded, then went into the kitchen.

I sat on the sofa near the side table.

The living room was simply furnished: a sofa accompanied by a coffee table, a single side-table on the right side of the sofa with a lamp on it, and two upholstered chairs—one chair sat opposite from where I was sitting and the other sat at a ninety-degree angle to the left of the sofa. A stand-up lamp stood beside it.

Nice, I thought.

To the left of the main entrance that led directly into the living room, there was a double-window that overlooked the street. The window was masked by a Venetian blind and dressed with short beige curtains.

The kitchen was through an open doorway on the right and the bathroom was probably in the hallway on the left where there were two doors, which indicated that there was only one bedroom.

She entered the living room and approached me. "Don't get up." She gave me a mug of hot coffee.

"May I ask you more about what you know about Cookie and . . . and Vietnam?" I shifted my position on the sofa from my left to my right side.

"Charles was career Army." She approached the upholstered chair opposite to where I was sitting.

"That explains it."

"Explains what?"

"His age."

"He did not make retirement."

"Because . . . because of the War?"

"Of course."

"Wounded?"

"No. Disillusioned," she answered in despair.

"Oh."

"I don't understand that, either. He was a staff sergeant."

"Really."

"He did not re-enlist when . . . when—well—the truth is I simply don't know what happened to him to cause him not to re-enlist."

"Were you married then?"

"Married after."

"And you met—?"

"Here. In Baltimore. At the V.A. Hospital."

"Oh."

She noted my confusion. "I'm a public administrator at the hospital."

"I see."

"But I don't know anything about the military. I do know he was a great guy."

"Was?"

She frowned. "After we were married for a while, I discovered that I did not know him or . . . or maybe he changed. I'm . . . I'm not sure. Anyway, he was in Vietnam twice. His second tour was in 1968 and '69."

"That's when I was there."

"I don't know what he was, what he did in . . . in the Army. Staff sergeant doesn't mean anything to me. I don't know what he did in the war." She sat down. "He's never talked about himself in it. He won't talk about himself in it."

"I see."

"Funny."

"What?"

"I wish he would talk about himself—in the War." She sipped her coffee. "He's a talker."

"I know."

"He talks endlessly about everything except . . . except, this nothing that he won't talk about."

"Nothing?"

"That's how he refers to it." She placed her coffee mug on the side table.

"The War."

"His presence in the War. Vietnam is always this . . . this hidden experience, this . . . this—nothing."

"Yes?" I whispered, encouraging her to continue.

She shook her head. "It's nothing, he keeps saying. And for a while, I thought it was Zen talk. For a while, I hoped it was his . . . his Zen Noir." She grimaced. "That was his term."

"Zen Noir."

"Yes." She smiled. "Clever." She frowned. "It's nothing, he keeps saying. I've lost hope."

I placed my coffee mug on a side table.

"But lately, lately that nothing has become something that he can't seem to live with anymore. Lately it's been leaking out of him through anger. Lately he hasn't been able to quietly carry it inside that place that won't let him talk directly about it." She sighed. "I don't know what's changed. He's changed. But I don't know *what's* changed."

"I understand that," I said.

She was still beautiful, despite the crack in her age caused by the sorrow of her relationship with Cookie. "Men. You men."

I reached for my coffee, but changed my mind.

"What's your story?" she asked.

I shrugged my shoulders.

She did not press me for an answer.

her emotions caged,
her mystery caught
in the commerce of nothing,
in the sincerity of something

CHAPTER 48

Misspelled Steps

I felt sad after reaching the corner of Teresa's street.

I felt sad. I had allowed Catherine to haunt my past. I had let Sandy walk out of my future.

I walked. I slipped on broken glass. I tripped on a street curb.

Baltimore's night bit into my soul and distracted me from my somberness. Vietnam. The sound of small arms fire in the distance of my mind accompanied me all the way to my hotel. The sounds came to a stop after I entered the room and turned on the television.

synopsis of despair
intensifying the struggle;
searching with misspelled steps
for that moon-stained mystic

CHAPTER 49

I'm in Disguise

A knock on my door awakened me from a troubled sleep. I had a difficult time rolling out of the bed onto my feet. I approached the door and opened it. "What the hell?"

Cookie stared at me with a square-rooted smile. "Hey." His orange cap was stretched over his bandaged head.

"Get in here." I pressed my left palm against my forehead in amazement as Cookie stepped into my room. "When did they release you?"

"Who said they did?"

"Your head wound—"

"Wasn't very serious."

"I see." I shut the door. Cookie sat at the foot of my bed.

I approached him. "What have you done to yourself?"

"I shaved off my beard."

"No kidding."

"I'm in disguise."

"Not with that orange cap perched on your bandaged head."

"Oh, well." He shrugged. "How do I look?"

"You . . . you look—alright."

"Liar."

Cookie's eyes were distant. His angular features were sharper and his pallor was ghostlike in appearance. His jeans needed washing, his sports jacket needed ironing, and his boots needed polishing.

"Okay," I said. "You look like hell."

Cookie stared at the floor for a long time. "First Recon. First Marine Division."

"Okay. And?"

"Your outfit in the 'Nam," he declared.

"Yeah. How did you know that?"

"Jansen."

"Oh."

"He told you about—"

"Vietnam. So?"

"You're a ghost."

"Look who's talking," I said.

"Look who's here looking for ghosts," he countered.

"I think I found one, Army Staff Sergeant Charles Patrick Anderson."

Cookie was startled. "Yeah. How did you know?"

"Teresa."

"Oh."

"Sixty-nine. Seventy. Like me. Right?"

"Right. Combat Infantry."

"Ahh. A grunt."

"Like you."

"I need coffee." I changed my shirt.

I approached the room's coffeemaker and inserted the complimentary coffee bag into the drip filter holder. I filled the pot with water, poured the water into the drip coffeemaker, and inserted the pot between the filter holder and the pot warmer. "You need coffee, too." I pressed the red button to start the coffeemaker. "How did you manage to leave the hospital without somebody challenging you?"

"Why must we have a conscience?" Cookie placed his hands on his thighs and slumped forward using his arms for support.

It was clear that Cookie was not going to give me straight answers. "I . . . I don't know."

I tore off the plastic from two Styrofoam coffee cups and placed them near the coffeemaker.

Cookie took a deep breath, then exhaled. "I don't want to have faith. I want God, not belief."

I poured myself some coffee before the coffee-maker finished brewing the pot. "I can't help you." I sipped my coffee. "Teresa can't help you."

"I tried to kill God."

"You tried to kill yourself."

"And darkness prevailed," he countered.

I sipped my coffee. "I believe in God, and there *is* no God."

Cookie scrutinized me. "And you can live with that?"

"It's a habit. You can understand that. The church is too powerful a force, too great a childhood influence for me to completely discard. I had to incorporate."

"That's a hell of a contradiction to live with."

"It's working for me—for now. Most people live with worse."

Cookie's ruined eyes deepened with thoughtfulness. "It's ridiculous."

"That's right."

"It's an absurd illusion."

"Yeah. The existentialists have it right. But I'm trying to live my life without believing in that illusion too hard."

"And you've known this all along."

I shrugged.

"Why didn't you say something to me?" he pressed.

"Because you had to arrive at your own understanding."

"Shit."

"How did I know you were going to shoot yourself?"

"Right." Cookie slumped his shoulders. "It wouldn't have helped. I wasn't listening."

"Are you listening now?"

"I'm trying to." He pressed the palms of his hands against his closed eyes. "God. And the War. And—Teresa. What a mess I've made of myself."

I thought about the mess I've made of myself as well.

I set down my coffee and poured him a cup. "Here."

Cookie accepted my offer.

I picked up my cup.

He sipped his coffee.

I stared at the floor.

upraised arm and clenched fist;

where is justice in pain?

a stranger among strangers;

is it wrong to be lost?

CHAPTER 50

Epiphany

Cookie had been in the bathroom for a long time.

I started to worry. I knocked on the door.

No answer.

"Cookie." I grabbed the doorknob, turned it, and discovered that it was unlocked. I pushed open the door too forcefully—it banged against the bathroom's wall. I stepped across the door's threshold.

Cookie was leaning against the bathroom sink, facing the mirror. He was unaffected by my clumsy intrusion. He peered at my reflection on the mirror, then bowed his head. Crazy thoughts apparently assaulted him.

I leaned against the door jamb.

Tears streamed down Cookie's face with the intensity of one who had an epiphany.

He unfurled a length of toilet paper and tore off several sheets from the roll. He blew his nose. He wiped his eyes with the back of his hands. He looked at me. "You're crazier than I am."

I was glad that he wasn't looking at me when I lied. "Yes."

seeing God
in different terms;
wanting freedom
from nothing

CHAPTER 51

Synopsis of Despair

I responded to a furtive knock on my hotel room door without peeking through the peephole. Teresa questioned me as soon as I pulled open the door and presented myself.

"Where is he?"

I stepped aside. "In here."

She entered the room.

Cookie was seated on the bed with his back toward us.

"How did you know he left the hospital?" I asked, as I shut the door.

"They called me. They wanted to know if he had come home."

"How did you know that he was—?"

"Where—where else would he go?" She glanced at Cookie. "What's wrong with him?"

"I don't know."

"Charles? Charles." She approached Cookie. She waved her right hand near Cookie's eyes to attract his attention.

He did not blink.

"Charles Patrick Anderson, talk to me," she pleaded.

No response.

I watched them. I held my breath. I remained still.

synopsis of despair, from
an uncertain distance;
afraid to approach
a fragile tableau

CHAPTER 52

Perspective in Blue

When I stepped back into the bedroom after having gone to the bathroom, I found Teresa sitting beside Cookie.

"What am I going to do?" she asked.

"Let him get some rest?"

"Help me take him home."

"Teresa." I shook my head. "You look tired."

"I am."

"Let him stay here with me tonight. Go home and get some rest."

She sighed. "Are you sure?"

"It's the right thing to do for now."

"The right thing to do," she whispered. She placed both hands on her lap.

perspective in blue,
a clinging contusion;
elliptical wisdom
etched upon parchment

CHAPTER 53

Under the Bridge

When I woke up, I discovered that I was alone.

I had not slept long in the upholstered chair, but it had been long enough for Cookie to leave without disturbing my slumber.

I stood up. "Damn." I noticed the hotel's notepad on my bed.

I picked up the notepad and then read what Cookie had written.

> *I will be under the bridge on my own terms. You*
> *know, like Zack and Fish, Largo and Jansen and—you.*
> *arrogant beauty*
> *thinking things will be*
> *carefully arranged*

I grabbed my jacket and made sure I had my wallet and hotel key.

I decided not to call Teresa.

anarchist universe
wailing through the haze;
fractured mindscape
bending in the maze

CHAPTER 54

Cityscape

Brooding buildings stooped beneath an orange moon, as I walked under a camouflaged sky with an unwrapped mind. I traveled along an avenue spread underneath an indifferent consciousness. I was closer to the sun's rise than to what was left of the moon's light. Protected business storefronts appeared uninviting through the steel of security mesh. Their overhead fluorescent lights rained harshness upon their display merchandise.

I hesitated before one of the storefront windows with its impersonal display of heaven hanging above it: a purple *Three for One Sale* sign held by a thin-fingered angel pointing at the store's unlit marquee.

I continued walking and thinking and remembering this city as a homeless man among other homeless men who once walked invisibly in the street. They were gone.

A truck rumbled by.

I jaywalked across the street on a diagonal and against the dark hour of approaching daybreak.

savage trucks
undo themselves;
crossing an uncharted
celestial boulevard

CHAPTER 55

Renga Party

I ignored the trash and the broken glass on the road, as I traveled on a thin line of memory to my curved destination. When I reached the outskirts of some-where at the end of a roadway that led to the foot of a partially constructed, abandoned truss bridge, I recognized the place. There was no traffic.

I walked off the road, then shuffled down the man-made depression that led me under the foot of the bridge. From the road's level to the bottom of the depression, poured concrete arced downward in one smooth broad sheet. The place was littered with rock, glass, and debris. I saw Cookie sitting on the ground; he was hugging himself, as if he were cold. He saw me.

"Look at you," he said.

I approached him. "I read your haiku."

"You were supposed to."

"Do you believe it?"

Cookie looked at the sky. He pulled down the brim of his cap to the top of his eyebrows.

ancient night
a star disappears into
the light of dawn

I studied the moment, pondered the haiku, then looked at the sky as well.

shooting star
slicing the autumn sky
into the present

Cookie nodded with approval. He stood up and whispered his connecting verse.

black and blue
reflections of a cold
moonlight

I stepped closer to him. Cookie waited for my response.

the sense of pain
the reading of a sutra
suddenly stops

"Look, man, I don't know what happened to you in the War. But whatever it is, you owe the guys who didn't make it back to live as good a life as you can."

"I'm trying."

"Bull. Grow up."

"You don't know me."

"That's right."

Then stop trying to help me, Llew."

"I'm not anymore."

"Then why are you still here?"

"Because . . . because of Teresa."

"She's nothing to you."

"She's a decent lady, and you're an idiot for not realizing that. In fact, I'm an idiot for not realizing my own life." I scanned the surrounding area. "I came here on a spiritual quest, and you know what I discovered?"

"What?"

"There's nowhere to go."

Cookie exhaled with contempt.

"The spirit—my spirit—is right here on earth. It's the here and the now—that's all we have. And that's good and beautiful and worth keeping alive for. There's nothing else, Cookie. A good life on earth is spirituality. There's no beginning or end to a quest because we are always in it." I stomped my right foot on the ground. "This, Cookie, this is the quest. It's called living on earth, man. Living." I stepped toward him. "Teresa loved you enough to track you down to my hotel room and you weren't smart enough to appreciate that you selfish bastard."

"I need a drink."

"No, you don't."

Cookie sighed.

"Stop worrying about where God's love was in Vietnam; worry about where Teresa's love is here. That's real." I placed my left hand on his shoulder. "Don't throw your life away."

Cookie grunted.

Jansen is dead. The War is over. Teresa loves you. I'm going home.

wanting back the night
and constellations;
the passionate face
of illumination

CHAPTER 56

Avoiding Violence

Cookie followed me up the depression. As soon as we reached the road at bridge level, I saw them: three unsavory characters.

"Watch it, Cookie," I whispered.

"Yeah, I see them," he said. "I know I've avoided telling you this, but . . . ."

"What?"

"There's more danger in these streets than when you were living here."

"Because . . . ."

"There are more criminals roaming the streets and living among the homeless now. Baltimore is not the same place."

"I know that. You can't go back. Remember?"

We veered toward the left and avoided them. We kept our heads down. We did not respond to

their calls. We intensified our pace toward downtown instead.

indolent strangers
penetrating the present;
avoiding violence, and
rough angles of the past

CHAPTER 57

Go Home

There was nobody on the streets at the hour near daybreak.

I convinced him to accompany me back to my hotel room after I bought us breakfast: hash browns and eggs and coffee.

The darkness of my room was welcomed. The *Do Not Disturb* sign on my door had kept out the maid service that would have drawn open the window curtains while straightening out the room.

I threw myself onto my unmade bed and exhaled some of my exhaustion.

Cookie stretched out on top of the other bed and groaned to convey his weariness. "What should I do, Llew? What?"

"Go home."

"Teresa doesn't want me."

"Go home anyway."

"I'm a bum."

"No, you're not."

"The War killed me."

"You're still breathing, God damn it."

Cookie did not respond.

I closed my eyes.

We drifted into an unsettled silence.

The rest of the day was consumed by a restless slumber.

constant rebirth
must be endured;
salvation must wait
for reality

CHAPTER 58

Promises on Earth

Cookie woke up feeling exhausted by a nightmare. I woke up feeling hungry.

"I need a drink," said Cookie.

"We need food," I countered.

Cookie went into the bathroom first.

I rolled out of bed, approached the window, and pulled open the curtain. The night presented an uncertain sky.

I heard Cookie taking a shower.

I wondered what the evening had in store for us.

without proof or
promises on earth—
heaven is not here,
not anywhere

CHAPTER 59

Don't Blame Vietnam

I stepped out of the bathroom after taking a shower.

Cookie was sitting on the edge of my bed, looking out the window. He was obviously waiting for me.

"I need a drink," he said.

"You need to straighten out your life, I told you."

"I don't have a life."

"I don't have a life."

I felt exasperated. "Don't blame Vietnam for that."

"I have nowhere to go."

"Now you're being stupid. I'll take you home."

"And I'll do what?"

"Apologize to your wife."

"She doesn't want my apology."

"You can still be a man." I slipped on my left shoe.

"I need a drink."

"You need something to eat." I put on my jacket.

"Yeah, yeah."

"Let's go. Come on."

traveling East and West
and not knowing if
all directions
lead to home

CHAPTER 60

Haunted Men

We walked into a clear and lovely evening when we left the hotel. The traffic was calm.

"I'm hungry," I declared.

Cookie grimaced. "I know a deli around the corner that serves decent pastrami sandwiches."

"That works for me," I said.

"Come on."

It was a short and pleasant walk.

The deli occupied the street-level corner of a three-story commercial building.

We entered the establishment.

The deli was plain and clean. There were a half-dozen Formica-top tables, each accommodated four diners on metal chairs. All the tables were dressed with salt and pepper shakers, a metal napkin dispenser, a small metal basket filled with sugar packets, four paper placemats, and four napkin-wrapped settings of silverware.

We placed our orders at the counter and watched the owner prepare our sandwiches. Then we carried our assembled meals on plastic trays to a table of our choosing; they were all unoccupied.

We ate in silence and listened to the steady traffic of customers picking up their take-out orders.

The deli served bottled beer, which improved the hot pastrami on rye and potato salad. I consumed all my food; Cookie ate half his sandwich and drank a beer.

"Are you happy now?" Cookie muttered.

"Eat your food."

"I'm eating, I'm eating." Cookie took a drink from his second beer instead.

I grabbed the half-sandwich that Cookie left on his plate after he pushed it away. "You need to eat."

"Half a sandwich is enough. Here." He pushed his dish of potato salad toward me.

"I will." I stabbed the white lump of potato salad with my fork. "I'm still hungry."

Cookie finished his second beer while I ate his food.

"What am I going to say to her that hasn't been said already?"

"I don't know what you mean by that?"

"We've talked a lot."

"Not about the War."

"Did she tell you that?"

"No. I made it up."

Cookie bit his lower lip. "I can't talk to her about . . . ." Cookie picked up his beer bottle. "Empty."

I finished his potato salad. "Whatever it is you've done, or seen, or permitted to happen—well, I know you can't talk about it."

Cookie placed the beer bottle on the table, then pushed it away. "Never a day goes by."

"I know."

"I'm sick to death of that damn war."

"It's who we are, man. It's what makes us special."

Cookie was pleasantly startled by my remark. "That's the first time anyone has ever said that to me."

"Well. You need to understand that, because the War inside of you is never going to go away. It's who you are—it's who we are." I pointed at the people who were standing at the deli's counter. "And those civilians over there—those . . . those citizens don't know anything. They don't even care."

Cookie nodded. "That's right."

"I don't have any answers, man."

Cookie became restless.

I stood up. "Let's go."

We left the deli and walked due north, northerly—toward Teresa.

haunted men
exhausted by memory;
commanding respect
with each broken step

CHAPTER 61

Discordant Cry

We climbed the porch steps and approached the front door of Cookie's row-house. "Are you going to be alright?"

"I believe in God, and there is no God."

"Is that going to work for you?"

Cookie shrugged. "It's thin."

"It's all I have to offer you."

Cookie stared at the door while we waited for Teresa to answer to my second knock.

The door opened.

"Oh, my God!" was her discordant cry.

She ushered us inside, then shut the door.

surviving
dissonant
riffs, into
her safety

CHAPTER 62

Hopeful

The talk was small and careful and hopeful. She insisted that we go into the kitchen. Then she indicated, by pointing at the chairs, for Cookie and I to sit down.

I glanced at Cookie. He glanced at Teresa.

"Wait here," she said.

Cookie eased into the other chair after I sat down. He appeared exhausted. Hopeful.

The kitchen was just big enough to accommodate a small table with two chairs positioned against the wall opposite the sink. There was a gas stove on the left side of the sink and a small counter with a drain board on the right side of it, with drawers beneath it and cabinets above it. On the wall opposite the counter stood a large refrigerator, which was nestled against that corner. The kitchen was clean and orderly but the appliances were old, the porcelain sink was stained, and the linoleum floor was cracked.

Teresa returned with a short stool and positioned it between us near the table. "I'll make coffee."

Cookie and I remained silent as we watched her. She served Cookie first. "Are you alright?"

"I believe in God," he said. "And there is no God."

Teresa glanced at me before she addressed him. "I don't care. If that will control your drinking. I don't care. If that will help you and help push Vietnam away. I don't care."

Cookie peered at her to express his determination.

She responded with a tired smile. She poured another cup of coffee and served it to me. "Go home, Llew."

I took a sip of my coffee. "Okay."

She poured herself a cup and caressed it with both hands. "I believe Cookie and I can handle it from here." She remained standing.

I took another sip of coffee.

"She's right," Cookie added. "We can take care of ourselves. There's nothing for you here."

"Go back home and figure out your life," she added. "Whatever that is."

"I can't argue that," I said. "I'm still on leave and, well, I'll need every bit of it to . . . to untangle my relationship with Sandy to see if . . . if, well—to see if there is going to be a Sandy in my life."

"I understand." She scrutinized Cookie. "I've run out of leave. I . . . I can't watch over you anymore. I've got to go back to work."

"I know."

She placed her coffee cup on the kitchen counter. "Then know this—this is our last chance."

"Right." Then he peered at me. "Thank you."

"I didn't do anything."

"I'm here, Llew. And Teresa made us coffee and . . . ."

I ceded to his gratitude with a nod.

their parting gift
a hopeful thank you;
in their world
the hour was closed

CHAPTER 63

Wife

I stared at my packed bag.

My hotel room felt particularly empty from where I sat—at the foot of my hotel room's bed.

I stood up and went into the bathroom. And when I started to gather the toiletries that remained in the bathroom counter, I glanced at my reflection in the bathroom mirror.

I paused for a longer look.

When my features came into focus, that image did not match the one I carried within myself.

My hair: grayer—faded, much like the fabric of . . . of my old furniture. Furniture I had clung to for years.

My God. Why had I resisted Sandy every time she mentioned buying a new sofa, a new table—new furniture? Why? Because it kept my world intact: Catherine's and mine.

slumber's caress:
the rise and the fall of
her slender breath

Yes. Catherine's image was part of that picture that I carried within myself.

Catherine: her face—youthful, beautiful; frozen in time.

her chest rises
to let her breaths fall
on my pillow

In the mirror, there—look: he was still counting the breaths of her past. Yes, that smooth faced boy-man with black hair. He was still present in the bathroom mirror, but with the sparkle of youth absent from his eyes.

I leaned closer to the mirror. I studied my eyes. I saw what I thought was a glimmer of wisdom.

Yes. I had challenged Cookie to make peace with Vietnam. I had told him that the War was what separated us from . . . from everybody else. It was always going to be a part of who we are, and we owed it to those whom we left behind to make the best of our lives.

And yet, I had not taken my own advice—when it came to my wife.

It was time, if it was not too late, to find Sandy—the woman whose life matched mine, year for year.

CHAPTER 64

Pancakes

I awoke at noon feeling as empty as my apartment. I sat up on my bed. I rubbed my eyes and remembered.

Yes, it all happened. Cookie and Teresa and Baltimore.

I got out of bed, took a shower, and got dressed. Then I decided to go out for coffee.

She saw me as soon as I stepped outside. She was standing in the parking lot.

"Hello, Llew."

"Sandy." I approached her.

We hugged.

"What are you doing here?" I asked.

"I . . . I wanted to see how you were."

"I'm better—now that you're here. How are you?"

"Glad to see you. Glad . . . glad to be home."

I was grateful for her response.

Sandy's beauty always surprised me: closely cut light-brown hair, gray eyes, fair complexion, delicate features. She possessed an air of feminine dignity. She wore a pair of black slacks and a green blouse. Her figure was shapely and well-proportioned; her movement effortless—her manner graceful.

"How is your mother?"

"I think she's relieved to have her own place back."

"I don't believe that."

"Then I'm the one relieved."

I chuckled. "Okay."

She responded to my chuckle with a broad smile. "Did you miss me?"

"Yes. Of course."

"I bought new furniture," Sandy announced. "Delivery is next week."

"You did?"

She placed her left hand on her hip to emphasis her declaration. "Yes."

"I know—it's time."

Sandy's left hand slipped off her hip and dissolved her akimbo attitude. "It has to be, Llew."

"I know."

"I can't be old furniture anymore."

"I . . . I realize that now."

"I'm glad."

I sighed. "Furniture."

She pursed her lips. "Identity."

"Of course."

Sandy laughed.

"What?"

"Aren't we a pair?"

"Of what?"

"Characters."

I grinned. "I love new furniture."

"Are you sure?"

"I know that my love has been old furniture for a long time."

She stepped toward me. "I'm not Catherine."

"That's right." I stepped toward her. "You're Sandra McKenna."

She touched my right shoulder. "I love you, Llew."

"And I love you."

I kissed her. She kissed me. We hugged.

"Have you had breakfast?" I asked.

She shook her head. She appeared to be on the edge of tears. She managed to direct a smile at me.

"Come on." I escorted her to the passenger side of my car, opened the door, and waited for her to get into the car. I shut the door, walked to the other side of the vehicle, opened the door, and sat behind the driver's wheel. "I need coffee."

"Me, too."

I slammed the door shut. "Pancakes."

"Pancakes."

I started the car and shifted the automatic trans-
mission into drive and my mind into the future.

our souls are
invisible
yet, wrapped
in thin paper

Author's Biography

D.S. Lliteras is the author of thirteen books that have received national and international acclaim. Some of his novels have been translated into Italian, Russian, and Japanese. His short stories and poetry have appeared in numerous national and international magazines, journals, and anthologies.

D.S. Lliteras enlisted in the U.S. Navy after high school and served in Vietnam as a combat corpsman attached to the First Reconnaissance Battalion, First Marine Division, earning a Bronze Star Medal (with Combat "V") for valor. While in-country, Lliteras completed twenty long-range reconnaissance patrols and eighty combat dives.

After his discharge in 1970, he enrolled at Florida State University where he received his Bachelor of Arts and Master of Fine Arts degrees.

Lliteras worked as a theatrical director until 1979 then quit directing and became a merchant sailor. In 1981, he earned a commission in the U.S. Navy and served as a Deep Sea Diving and Salvage Officer. After several years of service, which included extreme, arduous sea duty, Lliteras resigned his naval commission and became a professional fire fighter.

After retiring from the fire department, he has been able to devote his full time to writing fiction.

His Wikipedia address is *http://en.wikipedia.org/wiki/D._S._Lliteras.*

Also by D.S. Lliteras

Viet Man

Flames and Smoke Visible

The Master of Secrets

The Silence of John

Jerusalem's Rain

Judas the Gentile

The Thieves of Golgotha

613 West Jefferson

In a Warrior's Romance

In the Heart of Things

Into the Ashes

Half Hidden by Twilight

Praise for other books by D.S. Lliteras

Viet Man

"*Viet Man* is an "absorbing, gritty military novel . . . he wins the reader's admiration with his loyalty to and compassion for his battle-mauled patients . . . an accomplished novel."

—*Publishers Weekly*

[*Viet Man*] ". . . is forcefully written, and it has much to say about life and death and war and peace . . . Fine war fiction from a writer who's been there."

—*Booklist*

"This is a powerful novel, eloquent while using the simplest of vocabulary and poetic in its clear-eyed imagery. Read it. Your understanding of this tumultuous period of our history will be forever enriched."

—*Military Writers Society of America*
(MWSA Gold Medal Award Winner)

"What *Viet Man* offers us is not only a work worthy of literary accolades, but a tribute to a time when the world was confused and tenuous—and we have never been able to understand why, until now, where between the covers of this book we find our own Wilfred Owens. Highly Recommended."

—*Literary Aficionado* (Ontario, Canada)

"Lliteras may think he wrote a novel, but *Viet Man* is truth . . . Lliteras's ability to paint a visual image has you walking alongside him trying to survive. In spite of the brutal reality of Vietnam, there is an undeniable bond between brothers-in-arms . . . this is the game changer. Now you get Vietnam."

—*VietNow Magazine*

Flames and Smoke Visible

"[T]his brief glimpse into both the mundane and exciting moments in a firefighter's career is sobering."

—*Library Journal*

". . . Lliteras nicely mixes the quiet with the heart-pounding . . . *Flames and Smoke Visible* will light you up."

—Terri Schlichenmeyer, *TheBookwormSez*

"Lliteras has been at war on two fronts, fighting both enemy soldiers and raging fires, and there is a hard-earned wisdom in these true-life episodes that grips our attention."

—*Publishers Weekly*

"Lliteras takes the reader inside the dangerous job of firefighting with an intensity no other writer/fire-fighter I have read has done . . . a beautifully written, riveting account about this profession that is entertaining and also informs, instructs, and allows the reader access to the human heart."

—*The VVA Veteran*

Related Titles

If you enjoyed *Syllables of Rain,* you may also enjoy other Rainbow Ridge titles. Read more about them at www.rainbowridgebooks.com.

The Cosmic Internet: Explanations from the Other Side
by Frank DeMarco

Consciousness: Bridging the Gap Between Conventional Science and the New Super Science of Quantum Mechanics
by Eva Herr

Messiah's Handbook: Reminders for the Advanced Soul
by Richard Bach

Blue Sky, White Clouds
by Eliezer Sobel

Inner Vegas: Creating Miracles, Abundance, and Health
by Joe Gallenberger

When the Horses Whisper
by Rosalyn Berne

God's Message to the World: You've Got Me All Wrong
by Neale Donald Walsch

Conversations with God, Book 4: Awaken the Species
by Neale Donald Walsch

Rainbow Ridge Books publishes spiritual, metaphysical, and self-help titles, and is distributed by Square One Publishers in Garden City Park, New York.

To contact authors and editors, peruse our titles, and see submission guidelines, please visit our website at www.rainbowridgebooks.com.